HENRY

JAMES

RCY

TITLES AVAILABLE IN BUZZ BOOKS

THOMAS THE TANK ENGINE

1. Thomas in trouble
2. Toby and the Stout Gentleman
3. Percy runs away
4. Thomas and the Breakdown Train
5. Edward, Gordon and Henry
6. Thomas goes Fishing
7. Thomas down the Mine
8. James and the Troublesome Trucks
9. Gordon off the Rails
10. Thomas and Terence
11. James and the Tar Wagons
12. Thomas and Bertie
13. Thomas and the Trucks
14. Thomas's Christmas Party

FIREMAN SAM

1. Trevor's Trial Run
2. Norman's Spooky Night
3. A Bad Day for Dilys
4. Bella and the Bird's Nest
5. The Pride of Pontypandy
6. A Surprise for Sarah
7. Elvis's Experiment
8. Christmas in Pontypandy

TUGS

1. Kidnapped
2. Run Aground
3. Nothing to Declare
4. Treasure Hunt

BUGS BUNNY

1. Ali Baba Bunny
2. Knighty Knight Bugs
3. Broomstick Bunny
4. Mutiny on the Bunny

BARNEY

1. Barney and the Picnic
2. Barney's New Hair-Do
3. Barney Goes Shopping
4. Barney's Happy Christmas

MICRO MACHINES

1. Road Block
2. Hijack
3. Safe Breakers
4. Snowbound

GREMLINS

1. Don't Get Wet
2. Midnight Feast

First published 1990 by Buzz Books,
an imprint of the Octopus Publishing Group,
Michelin House, 81 Fulham Road, London SW3 6RB

LONDON MELBOURNE AUCKLAND

Copyright © William Heinemann Ltd 1990

All publishing rights: William Heinemann Ltd. All television
and merchandising rights licensed by William Heinemann Ltd
to Britt Allcroft (Thomas) Ltd exclusively, worldwide.

Photographs © Britt Allcroft (Thomas) Ltd 1985, 1986
Photographs by David Mitton, Kenny McArthur and
Terry Permane for Britt Allcroft's production of
Thomas the Tank Engine and Friends.

ISBN 1 85591 003 9

Printed and bound in the UK

THOMAS AND THE BREAKDOWN TRAIN

buzz books

Every day the Fat Controller came to the station to catch his train. He always walked over to have a word with Thomas the Tank Engine.

"Hello, Thomas," he said. "Remember to be patient. You can never be as strong and fast as Gordon, the big blue engine, but you can be a Really Useful Engine. Don't let those trucks tease you."

There were lots of trucks at the station. They were silly and noisy. They talked too much and played tricks on engines that they were not used to.

Thomas worked very hard, pushing and pulling the trucks into place and getting them ready for the big engines to take on long journeys.

There was also a small coach and two strange things that his driver called *cranes*.

"That's the breakdown train," he told
Thomas. "The cranes are for lifting heavy
things like engines and coaches and trucks."

One day, Thomas was very busy in the
yard. Suddenly, he heard an engine
whistling, "Help! Help!" When he looked
towards the line he saw a goods train come
rushing through, much too fast.

12

Thomas could see that it was James – and James looked very frightened. He was screaming and whistling. His brake blocks were on fire!

"They're pushing me! They're pushing me!" he panted.

But the trucks were laughing. They were having lots of fun with James. Poor James went faster and faster. He was still whistling and calling for help as he disappeared down the line.

"I'd like to teach those trucks a lesson," said Thomas.

Then came the alarm.

"James is off the line! Fetch the breakdown train – quickly!" shouted one of the men.

Thomas was coupled on to the breakdown train and off they went. Thomas worked his hardest.

"Hurry! Hurry! Hurry!" he puffed.

"Bother those trucks and their tricks. I hope poor James isn't hurt," said Thomas as he hurried along.

They found James at a bend in the line.
He was in a field with a cow looking at him.

James's driver and the fireman were feeling him all over to see if he was hurt.

"Never mind, James," they said. "It wasn't your fault. It was those wooden brakes they gave you. We always said they were no good."

Thomas pushed the breakdown train alongside James. Then he pulled the unhurt trucks out of the way.

"Oh dear! Oh dear!" they groaned.

"Serves you right. Serves you right," puffed Thomas. He was hard at work puffing backwards and forwards all afternoon.

"This'll teach you a lesson. This'll teach you a lesson," he told the trucks.

They left the broken trucks and then, with two cranes, they put James back on the rails. He tried to move, but he couldn't. So Thomas helped him back to the shed.

The Fat Controller was waiting anxiously for them. He smiled when he saw Thomas.

"Well, Thomas," he said. "I've heard all about it, and I'm very pleased with you. You are a Really Useful Engine!"

"James shall have some proper brakes and a new coat of paint," he said. "And Thomas, you shall have a branch line all to yourself!"

"Oh! Thank you, sir!" said Thomas, feeling very proud.

Now Thomas is as happy as can be. He has a branch line and two coaches called Annie and Clarabel. Annie can only take passengers and Clarabel can take passengers, luggage and a guard.

They are both old and need new paint, but Thomas puffs proudly backwards and forwards with them, all day.

He is never lonely. His friends, Edward and Henry, stop quite often to tell him the news.

Gordon, the biggest and proudest engine, is always in a hurry, but he never forgets to say, "Poop, poop," and Thomas always whistles, "Peep, peep," in return.

THOMAS

EDWARD

GORDON